ABOUT THIS BOOK

EINSTEIN ANDERSON Science Sleuth
Seymour Simon
Illustrated by Fred Winkowski

Adam Anderson is no ordinary sixth-grader—that's why
everyone calls him Einstein. He's such a whiz at science
that he can solve any mystery or unravel any puzzle.

Watch as he investigates a flying saucer, foils the school
bully, and discovers the secret of his archrival's incredible
shrinking machine. Then pit *your* brain against Einstein's
—and may the best scientist win!

"A winner!"   —Nancy Larrick, author of
                    A Parent's Guide to Children's Reading

"Entertaining"   —*School Library Journal*

EINSTEIN ANDERSON

Science Sleuth

Seymour Simon

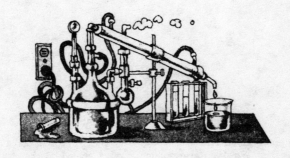

Illustrated by Fred Winkowski

A TRUMPET CLUB SPECIAL EDITION

For my sons,
Robert Paul and Michael Alan,
with love

Published by The Trumpet Club
666 Fifth Avenue, New York, New York 10103

Text copyright © Seymour Simon, 1980
Illustrations copyright © Viking Penguin Inc., 1980

ISBN 0-440-84849-0

This edition published by arrangement with Viking
Penguin, a division of Penguin Books USA Inc.
Set in Trump
Printed in the United States of America
January 1992

1 3 5 7 9 10 8 6 4 2
CWO

Contents

In this book Einstein Anderson solves puzzles by using his knowledge in these areas of science:

motion
friction
astronomy
animal behavior
chemistry
zoology
buoyancy
space science
sound and light

Einstein Anderson, Science Sleuth

1
The Frictionless
Roller Skates

It was the best day of the year. At least that's what Einstein Anderson thought.

School had let out yesterday in the town of Sparta—today was the beginning of summer vacation. Two months of sleeping late in the morning. Two months of doing what Einstein wanted to do, not what Ms. Sugar, his fifth-grade teacher last term, wanted him to do.

Einstein's real name was Adam. But nobody called him Adam, except his father and mother once in a while. Einstein had been interested in science for as long as he could remember. From an early age he had solved science problem after science problem that stumped even his teachers.

At the age of six Einstein had explained to Ms. Moore, his kindergarten teacher, how to use the chemical, cobalt chloride, to test for humidity in the air. At the age of seven Einstein had shown Ms. Patrick, his first-grade teacher, how to set up a balanced aquarium in the classroom. At the age of eight Einstein had built a model of a robot that won first prize at the state-wide science fair.

It was Ms. Moore who gave Adam the nickname of Einstein. Soon all his friends called him Einstein. Adam was proud of his nickname. He knew that Albert Einstein was the most famous scientist of the twentieth century. He had discovered many important things about the universe. His equation, $E=mc^2$, led to the understanding of atomic energy. Albert Einstein had been a gentle, kind man as well as a genius.

Einstein Anderson pushed his head deeper into his pillow. He guessed he would get up in another hour or so. That is, if he felt like getting up.

The phone downstairs began to ring. Einstein drowsily wished that someone would answer it. The ringing was keeping him awake. He opened one eye. Judging from the light in the room, he estimated it was 7:00 A.M. Where was Mom? Where was Dad? Where was his younger brother, Dennis?

Did they expect Einstein to get up and answer the phone on the first day of his vacation?

The phone stopped ringing. After a minute Dennis yelled that the call was for Einstein.

"Who is it?" Einstein called downstairs.

"It's Stanley," Dennis answered.

Stanley Roberts was an older, teenaged friend of Einstein's who was also very much into science.

Einstein put on his glasses, walked down the stairs, and picked up the phone sleepily.

"This had better be an emergency, Stanley," Einstein exclaimed as a way of greeting. "You know it's only seven in the morning and this is the first day of vacation!"

But he knew Stanley would pay no attention to his grumpiness. After all, Stanley was in high school.

"Einstein," Stanley said, "meet me in front of my house in half an hour. I have something to show you."

That really upset Einstein. "First of all," he said, "I don't want to go out so early in the morning. Second of all, if you have something to show me, why don't you bring it over here?"

As usual, Stanley ignored him. "See you in half an hour," he repeated and hung up before Einstein could say anything.

It must be another one of Stanley's crazy inventions, Einstein thought. But as long as I'm up, I guess I might as well see what he made this time.

Einstein remembered Stanley's last invention— an automatic fitting machine. A person stepped into the machine, and a computer was supposed to measure everything automatically, from shoe size, to belt size, to hat size. Stanley had persuaded Einstein to be the first person to step into the machine.

The machine worked fine. The only trouble was that Stanley had not been able to shut it off after Einstein had been measured. Einstein had been trapped for an hour while the machine kept mea-

suring him over and over again. Einstein liked Stanley but didn't exactly trust Stanley's crazy inventions.

Einstein washed and got dressed in jeans, T-shirt, and sneakers. The jeans were all raggedy at the knees, but they were Einstein's favorite. So far he had refused to throw them in the rag pile, despite his mother's pointed suggestions.

Einstein was an average-size twelve-year-old boy. His light brown eyes were a little nearsighted, and his glasses seemed a bit too big for his face. His eyes sometimes had a faraway look, as if he were thinking about some important problem in science. But Einstein was not always serious. He loved a good joke (or even a bad one) and liked to make puns, the worse the better.

Dr. Anderson, Einstein's father, looked surprised when his son walked into the kitchen and sat down at the table. He was just finishing breakfast and was about to leave for his office. Dr. Anderson was a veterinarian. He was often up and about before Einstein came for breakfast.

"To what do we owe the honor of your presence so early in the morning, Adam?" asked Dr. Anderson with a smile.

"I'm going over to see Stanley," said Einstein. "He called and asked me to come right over this morning." Einstein sniffed the air. "Any pancakes left, Mom?" he asked hopefully. "I just have time for a light breakfast."

Einstein walked over to the refrigerator and poured himself a glassful of orange juice. Then he popped two slices of bread into the toaster. Finally he poured himself a full bowl of milk and breakfast cereal and sat down to eat.

Mrs. Anderson looked on with amusement as she made another batch of pancakes. "I'm glad you're going to eat something," she said. "Too bad you don't have the time for a full breakfast."

Mrs. Anderson jotted down a note on a pad of paper while the pancakes sizzled. She worked as a writer and editor on the Sparta *Tribune*, one of the town's two newspapers. She often used the things her two boys did and said in humorous stories she wrote for the paper.

Einstein finished his "light" breakfast and walked over to Stanley's house. Einstein and Stanley lived in a section of Sparta that had a mixture of private homes and low-rise apartment houses. But there was still much undeveloped land around, with plenty of trees, woods, and open fields. Just outside of Sparta much of the land was used for farming, with a few office buildings scattered here and there. Most of the stores and office buildings were in the downtown part of Sparta.

It was a beautiful day. The early-morning traffic had let up and few cars passed by. The sound of a power-driven lawn mower in the distance mixed with the sound of insects. The smell of newly cut grass hung in the air.

Along the way to Stanley's house, Einstein looked at some red wood ants, *Formica rufa*, going into and out of an anthill. He watched a downy woodpecker tapping for insects along a branch of a sugar maple tree. He also threw some small granite rocks into the pond to test the strength of his pitching arm, and decided that the cumulus clouds in the blue sky meant a fair-weather day.

Einstein got to Stanley's house twenty-five minutes late. Stanley was fastening a pair of roller skates to his shoes when Einstein arrived. Stanley looked pointedly at his watch. Einstein paid no attention and just waited for Stanley to say something. Stanley was tall and thin. His long black hair was often falling over his eyes.

"Despite your lateness, Einstein, I'm going to show you my new invention."

"Oh, goody," Einstein said. "I hope it's something that prevents people from waking up other people when they want to sleep late."

Stanley didn't notice Einstein's tone of voice. He

stood up and started to roller skate in the street. "Look at these skates," he said proudly.

Einstein looked. "So," he said, "it's a pair of skates. I think J. L. Plimpton invented roller skates in 1863. You're more than a hundred years too late."

"He didn't invent skates like these," said Stanley in that slightly superior way of his. "These are roller skates that are frictionless. You know," he said as he skated back toward Einstein, "that friction is a force that resists an object moving over the surface of another object."

Einstein nodded impatiently. "Of course," he said.

But Stanley continued with his explanation. "Suppose two things are touching. When they move, they rub against each other. The rubbing causes the movement to slow down. We scientists call that friction. The smoother an object is, the less friction it causes.

"I used a special method to make the ball bearings in the skate wheel smooth. There is absolutely no friction when the wheels turn. One push and a person just keeps going."

Stanley sat down on the curb and held up one of the skates on his feet. He spun the wheels with his hand. They turned rapidly without making much

of a sound for several minutes until they began to slow down.

Stanley looked at Einstein and said, "What do you think of my frictionless roller skates? Maybe I should get a patent on the idea and sell it to a roller skate company."

"Your skates are terrific, Stanley," Einstein answered. He pushed back his glasses, which were slipping off the end of his nose. "But I'm afraid they are not frictionless."

"Come on, Einstein," said Stanley. "How can you know that without even trying on the skates?"

Can you solve the puzzle: How did Einstein know that Stanley's skates still had friction?

"Look at the skates," said Einstein. "They've stopped spinning."

"So what?" asked Stanley.

"But that's just it," said Einstein. "You started your skates spinning. If they were completely without friction, they would keep spinning forever. But even with a little friction, they will finally slow down and stop."

"Maybe I better keep working on the skates," said Stanley.

"I think you should invent something else," answered Einstein. "No one has ever been able to make a machine that's completely without friction. It's impossible to have two things touch each other with absolutely no friction."

"I guess you're right," said Stanley dejectedly. But then his face brightened. "Say, Einstein," he said, "I just fixed my automatic measuring machine. Do you want to try it out again?"

"When it comes to your inventions," said Einstein, "with friends like you I don't need enemies."

2

The Incredible
Shrinking Machine

Margaret Michaels was Einstein's good friend and arch rival. Science was their favorite subject. Einstein and Margaret were always talking about important things like atoms, planets, and who was the best science student.

Margaret's mother didn't quite know what to make of her daughter. Mrs. Michaels had wanted Margaret to take ballet classes on Saturday mornings. Margaret had insisted that she wanted to be in the Saturday Science Experimenters Club.

Mrs. Michaels thought that animals were nice when they were outside of her house. Margaret thought that animals were nice both outside and inside the house. She had a pet springer spaniel named Nova, two pet cats named Orville and Wilbur, a pet gerbil named Sammy, and assorted tropical fish. She hadn't named them yet.

Mrs. Michaels liked to listen to classical music. Margaret liked to listen to jazz. Mrs. Michaels was a member of the Sparta Choral Singing Society. Margaret couldn't sing a note in tune. But despite all the differences between them, Mrs. Michaels was very proud of her daughter's doings and boasted about her whenever she had the chance.

Margaret had left to visit her aunt for a week as soon as school was let out for the summer. Einstein knew that Margaret was back and wondered why she hadn't called him. Finally he decided to call and find out.

"Hello, Margaret, what's happening? How is your aunt? How come you didn't call?"

"Einstein," Margaret said, "I was just about to call you. Aunt Bess drove me home two days ago and stayed to visit my parents. She's going to drive back tomorrow, and she said it would be O.K. if I invited a friend to her house for the weekend. She's a biology professor at State University and has all kinds of science stuff at her house that you might like to see. How would you like to go?"

Einstein was about to refuse because his family

was going to the beach on Sunday, when Margaret continued.

"Also, I have a science puzzle to show you at Aunt Bess's that even the great Einstein Anderson can't solve."

Well, that changed everything. Einstein couldn't turn down a science challenge from Margaret, so he agreed to go. He spent the rest of the day playing baseball with some classmates and wondering about the puzzle that Margaret had mentioned.

Einstein and Margaret were driven by Aunt Bess early in the morning on Saturday. They arrived at Remsen, a town near the State University, just after 8:00 A.M. Aunt Bess's house was in a sort of clearing surrounded by trees. Instead of first going inside, Margaret led Einstein behind the house and down a twisting path in the woods.

Hidden from the house at the end of the path was a small shack with a bright yellow door. The early-morning sun shone directly on the yellow door and made it look almost like gold.

Margaret unlocked the yellow door and motioned Einstein inside. Einstein noticed that the single room they entered had no other doors and only one small window. The only objects in the room were a large stone table and a small black box sitting on the table.

"Einstein, look over the stone table closely,"

Margaret said. "It was put together right in this room. You can see that it is too big to pass through the door or the window. You would have to break it into little pieces to get it out of the room."

Einstein checked the table carefully. He could see that what Margaret said was true. You would need a bulldozer to break up that old stone table.

"I'm now going to switch on my incredible shrinking machine," said Margaret. She flipped a switch on the side of the little black box. Nothing much happened except that the black box sort of burped once and then was quiet.

Margaret motioned Einstein to follow her out. "We'll have to leave the room so as not to shrink ourselves," she said. "But when we come back in a few hours, the table will be gone without a trace. The incredible shrinking machine will have reduced it down to the size of an atom."

Margaret led Einstein back to Aunt Bess's house. For the rest of the day Einstein and Margaret experimented with chemical indicators such as litmus and brom thymol blue. They used a microscope to look at the protozoa in a drop of pond water. They fed food pellets to Aunt Bess's laboratory white mice. Lunch for Einstein and Margaret was peanut butter and jelly sandwiches.

Aunt Bess started an outdoor barbecue going late in the afternoon. They had grilled hamburgers, newly picked corn, a fresh tomato salad, and watermelon for dessert. It was all delicious and they didn't finish washing and straightening up till eight o'clock.

It was twilight when Margaret led Einstein back by a different path to the shack. They arrived just as the setting sun shone directly on the yellow door, turning it golden, just as it had done in the morning.

Margaret unlocked the door and they went inside. The room looked almost the same: one door, one small window, and one small black box. But the big stone table was gone. Nothing, not even a chip of stone, remained on the floor.

At first Einstein couldn't believe his eyes. Margaret might really stump him this time. How could that big stone table just disappear? Had Margaret really invented a shrinking machine?

Margaret smiled at the look on Einstein's face. "Well," she asked, "what do you think of my incredible shrinking machine?"

Einstein was quiet for a few minutes. Then his face changed and he began to laugh. He pushed back his glasses, which had slipped down. "You almost had me there for a minute, Margaret," he said. "I think I know what happened to the table. And if I'm correct, there is no such thing as an incredible shrinking machine."

Can you solve the puzzle: What do you think happened to the table?

"The key to the puzzle," Einstein began his explanation, "is the sun."

"The sun!" Margaret exclaimed. "What does the sun have to do with the shrinking machine?"

"You know that the sun rises in the east in the morning and sets in the west in the evening," Einstein explained. "Yet both the rising sun and the setting sun shone directly on the yellow door. That's impossible."

"So what's the answer?" Margaret asked.

"Simple," Einstein said. "There must be two doors and two rooms in the shack, one in back and one in front. The sun shone on one door in the morning and on the other door in the afternoon. You must have taken me into one room in the morning but into the other room in the afternoon. The first room contained the stone table. The other room didn't have anything in it."

"You're right," said Margaret.

They left the shack and started back to the

house. "I see that I made one mistake," Margaret said, shaking her head.

"What's that?" Einstein asked.

"I should have shown you my incredible shrinking machine on a cloudy day."

"Right," said Einstein. "Your machine had me in the dark for a while. But it was the sun that let me see the light."

3

The Howling Dog

Einstein was looking at some photographs of Jupiter showing the giant red spot on the planet's surface, when his eight-year-old brother Dennis burst into his room. Dennis had a scraped knee and an eye that was beginning to puff up.

"What happened to you?" Einstein asked.

"I just had a fight with my ex-friend Chuck," Dennis said. "He wanted to use my baseball glove and I told him he couldn't. So he grabbed the glove and I punched him. Then he started to hit me, but I got my glove back anyway. Chuck is bigger than I am, but you're bigger than he is. So I want you to go out and beat him up."

"Not so fast, Dennis," Einstein said. "I'm sorry Chuck hit you, but after all you hit him first. He shouldn't have grabbed your glove, but maybe you could have handled him in another way. After all, size and brains don't always go together."

"Well, what should I do?" asked Dennis.

"Maybe you can explain to him that your glove is new and that you are just working in the pocket. That way you can still remain friends with him without lending your glove."

"Do you think that will work?"

"I don't know," said Einstein, "but you can try. Just like I try to handle Pat Burns in my class. I could fight him if I had to, but I'd rather handle him with my brains."

"Who's Pat Burns?" asked Dennis.

"Pat is the biggest kid in my class. He's also the meanest. Everybody calls him Pat the Brat. He's got a friend named Herman who's the second meanest kid in the class. The best way to handle them is by thinking, not by fighting."

Just then the front doorbell rang. When Einstein went down to open the door, he was surprised to see the person he'd just been talking about—Pat the Brat.

Pat held a leash in his hand. At the other end of the leash was a large, brown mixed-breed dog. The dog growled when Einstein opened the door.

Einstein looked at Pat, then at the dog, then back at Pat.

"Hello, Pat. How are things?"

When Einstein leaned forward to stroke the dog on the head, the dog suddenly began to howl. Einstein leaped back. He was so startled that his glasses slipped down to the end of his nose. He pushed them back and asked, "Why is that dog howling like that?"

Pat laughed in a nasty way.

"Einstein," Pat said, "this is my dog, Rocky. Say hello to Rocky."

"Hello, Rocky," Einstein said.

Rocky kept on howling.

Einstein looked back at Pat. "Well, it's been nice having this chat with you and Rocky, but I got to go now. Be seeing you."

"Just a minute," Pat said. "I want to talk to you."

"I really got to go, Pat. Maybe some other time."

"Now," said Pat, and he clenched his fist slightly.

"Right," Einstein said with a sigh. "I just remembered that I do have the time to talk to you now."

Pat sat down on the front steps. He motioned Einstein to sit down next to him. Then he pointed his finger at Rocky. Rocky suddenly stopped his howling.

Despite himself Einstein became very much interested. "How did you do that, Pat?" he asked. "You just pointed your finger at the dog and he stopped howling. What's the trick?"

"That's for you to figure out, Einstein," Pat said with a sly smile. "You're supposed to be the genius in the class. So we're going to play a little guessing game. The winner gets to punch the loser five times on the arm. Ready to play?"

"I don't think I want to play," said Einstein. "I've really got to go. . . ."

"Either play now or pay now," said Pat, punching his right fist into his left hand.

"Right," said Einstein. Pat wasn't smart but he was strong. It was easier to outwit Pat than to fight him. "I always like a good game. What are the rules?"

"The rules are simple," said Pat, "All you have to do is explain to me how I can make Rocky howl or stop howling. Like this."

Pat pointed his finger at Rocky. The dog began to howl. Pat pointed his finger again. The dog stopped howling. "Try to make the dog howl, Einstein," said Pat.

Einstein pointed his finger at Rocky. The dog

just yawned. Einstein pointed his finger again. This time Rocky scratched his ear with his hind leg.

"I'll give you an hour to think it over," said Pat. "I'll be back with my pal Herman so he can be a witness when the winner collects."

Pat turned and led Rocky away. He looked back at Einstein over his shoulder and said, "Remember, one hour."

Einstein watched them walk down the street. Just before they got to the end of the block, he saw Herman jump out of some bushes and join Pat and the dog.

Einstein whipped out his pocket binoculars and saw Herman take a shiny object out of his mouth and put it in his pocket. The shiny object was a whistle. But had Herman been blowing a whistle? Einstein hadn't heard one.

Einstein sat down on the steps. His glasses slipped down again, but he didn't notice. He was trying to remember something that his father had told him about animals.

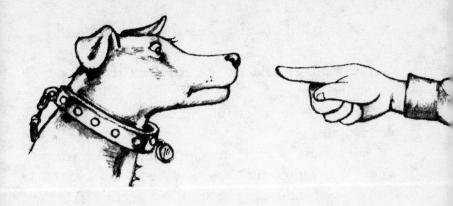

Pat, Herman, and Rocky returned to Einstein's house in an hour. Pat spoke first. "Ready to pay off now, Einstein?" he asked.

"First I'd like you to meet my kid brother, Dennis. Dennis, say hello to Pat and Herman."

"Hello," Dennis said.

"Hello, kid," Pat said. Herman didn't say anything. "You ready now, Einstein?" Pat asked.

"Are you sure you want to go through with this game?" asked Einstein.

"Sure, I'm sure," Pat said. "You trying to back out of it?"

"No," Einstein said. "I just want you to remember that the arm punches were your idea."

"I remember," Pat said. "Ready to get hit?"

"Not so fast," Einstein replied. "I think I know how you got the dog to howl. And if I'm right, you're the one who will have to pay off."

Can you solve the puzzle: How did Pat get Rocky to howl?

"I'm waiting," said Pat. "And I don't think you know the answer."

"That's the trouble, Pat," Einstein said. "You don't think."

"You're just wasting time, Einstein," Herman said. "You really don't know why Rocky howled."

"Oh—you think I'm just whistling in the dark?" asked Einstein.

"Whistling," Herman said, suddenly looking uncomfortable. "What's that got to do with it?"

"Oh, whistling has a lot to do with it," Einstein answered. "For example, let's take the whistle you have in your pocket. It's what's called a dog whistle. A dog whistle is so high-pitched that people can't hear the sound, but dogs can hear it even from a distance."

Herman looked at Pat. "I guess he knows how we did it," he said.

"I think I do," Einstein said. "You must have trained Rocky to howl whenever he heard the whistle and to stop when the whistle stopped. Herman, you were watching Pat from behind the bushes. Whenever you saw Pat point at Rocky, you blew the whistle and Rocky howled. But when I pointed at Rocky, you didn't blow the whistle and Rocky didn't howl."

"O.K., Einstein," Pat said. "You beat me this

time. But wait until next time." He pointed to his arm. "Are you going to collect your punches?"

"I'll take an IOU on them, Pat," Einstein said. "I'll tell you a joke instead. Why is your dog like a tree?"

"Why?" Pat asked.

"Because they both have a bark."

"I think Pat would rather be punched," Dennis said.

4
The Universal Solvent

Stanley looked excited when he met Einstein at the door of Stanley's house. Stanley's hair fell over his eyes. He didn't even get angry at Einstein for being half an hour late.

"This time I've invented something *really* fantastic," Stanley said. "Come up to the laboratory and I'll show you, Einstein."

Stanley turned and hurried up the stairs. His "laboratory" was really the attic room that his Mom and Dad had permitted him to use for his experiments. Einstein, who had been there many times, knew that it was overflowing with all kinds of . . . well, Stanley called it scientific apparatus.

When Stanley opened the attic door, the laboratory was in more of a mess than usual. Flasks filled with red, green, and blue liquids bubbled away. A maze of glass and plastic tubing connected the beakers one to another.

There was a peculiar odor in the room. Stanley said it was a perfume that he was working on to attract girl friends, but to Einstein it smelled like skunk. He decided not to mention this to Stanley, however.

At the end of the maze of tubing sat a small beaker half-filled with a clear red liquid. Stanley pointed to the beaker. "That's it," he said proudly. As he spoke, another drop of red liquid plopped into the beaker.

"What is it?" Einstein looked at the beaker curiously. "That looks like a glass of cherry soda pop to me."

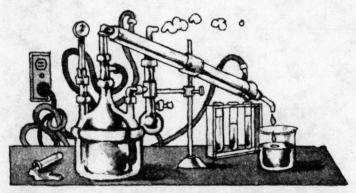

Stanley laughed in his best imitation of a mad scientist. "It *looks* like soda pop," he declared, rubbing his hands together gleefully, "but that liquid is the first universal solvent ever made."

"Oh," Einstein said. "That's great. Another one of your important scientific breakthroughs?"

"You know what a solvent is, don't you, Einstein?"

Without waiting for Einstein to say yes, Stanley explained. "A solvent is a liquid that dissolves another substance. For example, water dissolves sugar, salt, and many other things. We call that a solution of sugar, salt, or whatever is dissolved."

"I know," said Einstein. "In fact, water is an excellent solvent. Give it enough time and it can dissolve almost anything. You might even call it a kind of universal solvent."

"But that's just it," Stanley said in that schoolteacher voice he sometimes used. "Water doesn't dissolve *everything*. For example, water doesn't dissolve oil or fingernail polish. But you can use turpentine to dissolve oil, and nail polish remover to dissolve nail polish. There are lots of different solvents for different things. But my solvent dissolves anything."

"Right," Einstein said. "Let's see your solvent work."

Stanley took a piece of plastic and placed it in the beaker. He stirred it around with a glass rod. It got smaller and smaller. After a few minutes the piece of plastic had dissolved.

Einstein was impressed. He looked closely at the beaker.

Stanley looked over at Einstein and said, "Would you like me to dissolve your shirt?"

"Stanley," Einstein said, "I'd give the shirt off my back for a real scientific breakthrough, but suppose you try to dissolve some other things first."

"What would you like me to dissolve?" Stanley asked.

Einstein looked around the laboratory. "Try a

piece of chalk," he said, "and some linseed oil and some borax." Einstein knew that the chemicals he had chosen were only slightly soluble in water.

"Sure," Stanley said. He set up three more beakers with the red liquid. He dropped the chalk into one beaker and each of the other chemicals into the other two beakers. This time it took somewhat longer for anything to happen. But sure enough the chalk and the chemicals slowly began to dissolve.

Einstein looked thoughtful. He picked up each beaker of red liquid and looked at it carefully. Finally he pushed his glasses back onto his nose and smiled.

"That cherry soda you made may dissolve lots of things, but I wouldn't go to the patent office just yet. It is not a universal solvent. If it were, you would be in lots of trouble."

Can you solve the puzzle: How did Einstein know that Stanley had not invented a universal solvent? And what did he mean by saying that Stanley would be in lots of trouble if he did?

"What kind of trouble?" asked Stanley. "You mean with the government?"

"Not exactly the government," Einstein answered. "More like your parents . . . and anyone standing on the floor below us."

"What are you talking about, Einstein?"

"Just this," Einstein said. "A real universal solvent will dissolve anything, even glass. So if your cherry soda were a universal solvent it would dissolve the glass beaker and the stirring rod. No container could hold it. It would dissolve anything it touched, including the attic floor and anybody on the floors below as well."

Stanley slowly nodded. "I guess you're right, Einstein," he said.

Einstein smiled. "Look at it this way," he said. "It's better to solve a puzzle than to dis-solve an attic floor."

5
The Museum of Strange Objects

The circus came to Einstein's town the third week in July. Einstein took his brother, Dennis. They enjoyed seeing the lion tamer, the trapeze artists, the clowns, and all the other acts in the big top. When the show was over, they decided to see some of the exhibits in the sideshows.

The sideshows were set up in a series of small tents just behind the big top. The tents were set up to display all kinds of people with strange talents, such as a strong man, a fat lady, a sword swallower, a man who walked on fire, and someone who could tell your fortune just by "feeling the bumps on your head."

"How can you tell a person's fortune just by feeling the bumps on his head?" Dennis asked.

"It's about as accurate as telling a person's fortune by reading his palm or with a crystal ball or by the stars," Einstein said.

"You mean you don't believe in the stars?" Dennis asked.

"I believe in the stars," Einstein answered. "And also in planets, comets, meteors, nebulae, and galaxies. But somehow I find it difficult to believe that my lucky day depends upon groups of stars millions and millions of miles beyond the earth."

"I see what you mean," said Dennis.

"Well, I hope I didn't *star*-tle you," Einstein said.

"Ugh," said Dennis.

The circus also had food stands, rides, and games. Einstein and Dennis each ate a hot dog, a hamburger, French fries, a shake, and cotton candy, rode the roller coaster three times, and tried to ring a bell with a sledgehammer.

Einstein could hardly lift the hammer over his head. When he let the hammer drop, the chart read, "Weakling."

Dennis laughed, but when he tried the game, he didn't do any better. Einstein decided not to laugh when he saw the look on his brother's face.

The boys were walking out of the sideshow and

about to leave when they passed a tent that had a curious sign. The sign read, "The Museum of Strange Objects." A man standing in front was trying to get people to enter. He spoke through a megaphone. "Ten-dollar reward to anyone who can prove any of the objects inside is a fake."

Einstein said, "Let's go in and see what they have, Dennis. Maybe we can get that reward."

The boys walked over and checked the price of admission. It was fifty cents for each of them. Dennis reached into his pocket and counted the money he had left.

"I only have a little over a dollar left," Dennis said. "Maybe everything in there is real. Even if it isn't, how can we prove it? I think we should spend the money for ice cream."

Usually Einstein loved ice cream, but for some reason his stomach wasn't feeling too good just at that moment.

"Come on, Dennis," he said, "let's take a chance. If we get the reward, you can buy all the ice cream you want."

Dennis thought it over and then decided. "We'll go into the museum, Einstein, but I hope you can prove one of the things in there is a fake."

Inside the tent, several tables had been set up. On the tables were several dozen objects, ranging

EGGS

SPACE MAN'S SHOES

SKIN OF
20 FT. PYTHON

from eggs to rocks to shoes. Each object had a small typed label in front of it. The labels told a story about each of the objects.

Einstein and Dennis walked around and looked at each of the objects. There were exhibits of "moon rocks," "spaceman's shoes," and the "nose cone of a recovered rocket." There were large eggshells that, according to their labels, came from "a golden eagle," "the turkey vulture," and "the big brown bat." There were also some turtle eggs and the skin of a "twenty-foot-long python."

On another table was a collection of broken pieces of pottery that had been found "in a buried Indian village in the rain forests of Central America." The table also held several pieces of polished rock. The sign with the rocks read that they "had once been a tree trunk that had changed to stone over thousands of years."

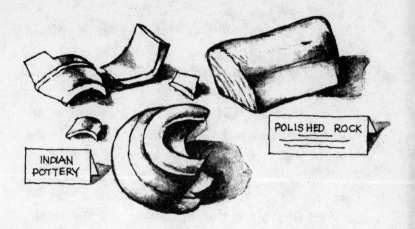

INDIAN POTTERY

POLISHED ROCK

Dennis picked up one of the pieces of rock. "This probably is a fake," he said. "Who ever heard of a tree that became a rock?"

Einstein looked at the rock carefully and then stared at Dennis. "Better a rock tree than a rock head," he said meaningfully.

"Very funny," said Dennis. But he didn't laugh.

As they kept walking around the room, Dennis seemed to be getting angry. "I'm getting very hungry, Einstein," he said. "I hope you can prove that something here is a fake. Is the rock a fake, or are all the objects real?"

"Oh, there's no problem about that," said Einstein. "At least one of the objects is obviously not what it says."

Can you solve the puzzle: Which object was a fake?

"I still think those tree rocks are a fake," Dennis said.

"I'm afraid not," said Einstein. "Those rocks are called petrified wood. They're usually found in the form of logs, tree trunks, and stumps. Over thousands of years each wood cell is replaced by a chemical called silica. Silica turns into a rock."

"Well, if it's not the rocks, then it must be the python's skin," Dennis said. "Who ever heard of a twenty-foot-long snake?"

"I have," Einstein said. "Pythons can grow to a length of more than *thirty* feet."

"Then which exhibit is a fake?" Dennis asked.

"The one object that is surely a fake is the brown bat's eggshell," Einstein said.

"How do you know?" Dennis asked.

"Because bats are flying mammals, not birds. Their wings are really arms with long fingers. A thin, furry skin stretched between the fingers forms the wing. And of course bats don't lay eggs like birds. Bats, like other mammals, give birth to living young." Einstein grinned. "You might say that the museum got its eggs scrambled."

"That reminds me," Dennis said. "I'm hungry."

6

The Weight Lifting
Contest

It was a real scorcher, the hottest day of the summer so far. Einstein had gotten out of bed early (a bit grumpily because he was still sleepy), packed his swimming suit, towel, and lunch. The rest of the family was just getting up when he went off to meet Margaret at the bus stop. They were going to the town beach.

The bus made its way through Sparta, stopping at every other street corner. Most of the passengers who got on the bus were kids headed for the beach. Soon the bus was filled to overflowing. Everybody was chattering away and happy at the thought of getting into the water and cooling off.

Einstein and Margaret were busy in conversation with each other and with friends seated nearby. Suddenly Margaret poked Einstein in the ribs.

Einstein jumped. "What did you do that for, Margaret?" he asked, rubbing his side.

Margaret pointed to two kids who had just boarded the bus and were making their way up the crowded aisle. "Look who's there," she said. "Everybody's favorite people, Pat the Brat and his shadow, Herman."

Einstein slunk down in his seat. "I hope they don't see me," he said. "The last time I saw Pat I won five arm punches because I knew why his dog howled."

Margaret shook her head in bewilderment. "What are you talking about? What does a howling dog have to do with five arm punches and Pat?"

Einstein didn't answer because just then Pat and Herman noticed him and came over.

Pat stood over him and glared down. "Well, if it isn't the genius, Einstein. I didn't know you were going to the beach today. I'll have to think up a contest. One that has ten arm punches as a prize. And this contest is one I'm going to win because it's not going to have any brains in it."

"That's the only kind of contest you have any chance of winning, Pat," Margaret said.

Pat glared at Margaret but didn't answer. The first and last time he had picked on Margaret, she had socked him a good one in the eye. As a result he had gone around with a black eye for a week.

Pat told everybody that he had bumped into a doorknob, until someone said, "Yeah, at the end of Margaret's fist." After that, Pat left Margaret strictly alone.

"I'll see you on the beach," Pat said to Einstein.

"Sure," Einstein said, "we'll be looking for you. ... And then going the other way," he added under his breath. Einstein wasn't afraid of Pat; he just saw no reason to fight with him.

The bus stopped at the beach. Kids scattered in all directions. Soon there were people swimming, people eating, people playing ball, and people sun-

ning themselves. Everybody was in a happy mood
... except when they spotted Pat and Herman
coming toward them.

Pat and Herman walked up to where Einstein
and Margaret were building a sand castle at the
edge of the water.

Pat was about to step on the castle when he noticed the look in Margaret's eyes. He took a step
back and then spoke to Einstein.

"Einstein, this is the contest that me and you
are going to have. Whoever can lift the heaviest

weight gets to punch the loser in the arm ten times. Ready?"

Einstein looked at the water lapping at his feet. He pushed back his glasses and thought about it for a minute.

"It's kind of a silly contest," said Einstein. "But I'm willing to try it with a few conditions."

"What kind of conditions?" asked Pat.

"First of all, each person gets only one chance to lift the heaviest weight he can find. Second, he can lift the weight any place he wants." Einstein saw Margaret begin to smile.

Pat thought about that for a while. What difference would it make where a person lifted a weight? Finally he said, "O.K., Einstein, you're on. The weight that I'm going to lift is you."

Pat went over to Einstein and placed his hands under Einstein's armpits. Grunting with the strain, he slowly lifted Einstein off the sand of the beach.

"Now it's your turn," Pat said nastily. "Who are you going to lift? Me?"

"That's exactly who I'm going to lift," Einstein said. "Just step over here."

Can you solve the puzzle: How could Einstein lift Pat, who was heavier? What difference could it make where Einstein did the lifting?

"Step over where?" Pat asked.

"Into the water," Einstein said. "Follow me into the water until I tell you to stop."

Einstein walked into the water, with Pat following him. Einstein stopped when the water was about as deep as Pat's neck. Then he turned to Pat and said, "Here's where I'm going to lift you." Einstein put his arms around Pat and lifted him with ease.

Herman was watching all this from the beach. His mouth dropped open when he saw Einstein lift Pat. "How could you lift Pat so easily?" he asked.

"Because Pat weighs less in water than he does in air," explained Einstein. "Water has a lifting force called buoyancy. As long as most of Pat's body is below the water, it's easy to lift him. It just proves that you need brains as well as strength when you try to do anything."

"O.K., Einstein, you can put me down now," said Pat.

Einstein smiled. "I think I already put you down, Pat," he said as he released his hold.

7

The Flying Saucer People

Einstein had just come home from the beach when his mother phoned him from her office at the Sparta *Tribune*.

"I'm glad you're home, Adam," said Mrs. Anderson. "I have a favor to ask you."

"Sure, Mom," Einstein said. "What can I do you for?" Einstein liked to mix up his words. It was unfortunate, he felt, that nobody else liked it.

"Adam, there's someone visiting Sparta I want to interview for the newspaper. I'm going to invite him to the house for dinner this evening. And I'd like you to be around when I do the interview."

"Who's the person? And why do you want me to be around? Is there something wrong?"

"His name is Mr. Janus," Mrs. Anderson answered. "He's writing a book about something that happened to him. Or at least that he claims happened to him."

"What happened to him? What do you want me to do when he comes? Do you think he's not telling the truth? Is it something about science?" Einstein asked all the questions in a rush.

"Just hold on a minute and I'll tell you," his mother said with a laugh. "Janus says he was walking along a country road just outside of Sparta when he saw a flying saucer. The saucer landed and some little people with big heads came out and greeted him."

"Wow!" Einstein exclaimed. "A close encounter of the third kind. What else happened?"

"Janus says that the saucer people were able to talk to him in English with some kind of translation machine they carried. They asked him to go aboard their ship and took him to their base on the far side of the moon. They kept him there for a few days and then took him back and released him."

"That really sounds weird," Einstein said. "Do you believe his story?"

"That's why I'd like you to be around," Mrs. Anderson answered. "He sounds sincere, but he may just be trying to get publicity for his book. I'd like you to listen to what he has to say and then tell me in private whether he's made any scientific mistakes."

Einstein readily agreed. He loved reading science fiction stories, though he had his doubts about flying saucers.

Mr. Janus turned out to be a long, thin man with sharp features. His eyes were black and piercing. All through dinner he talked about his experiences with the saucer people. He said that they were about three feet tall with the general shape of humans. They had a head, two arms, and two legs. Their skin was a faint greenish color that seemed to glow. Their eyes were very round with no pupils, and their ears were pointed.

Einstein listened closely, but he could not make up his mind one way or another. If you believed in saucers, he thought, then there was nothing scientifically wrong in anything Mr. Janus was saying.

After dinner Dr. Anderson said that he and Dennis would do the dishes. Dennis seemed to be about to protest, but Dr. Anderson gave him a look. Then Mrs. Anderson led Mr. Janus and Einstein into the den and shut the door.

"Would you continue with your story, Mr. Janus?" asked Mrs. Anderson. "You had just gotten to the part where the saucer people had given you a space suit and you were walking on the moon."

"The moon's surface was dusty and rocky," Mr. Janus said. "You know that there's no water or air on the moon. The temperature in the sunlight was over a hundred degrees Celsius. That's hot enough to boil water, if there was any. It's a good thing that the suit's air conditioning was working so well.

"The saucer people walked me over to a hill. When we got closer, I could hear a hammering going on behind the hill. It was not difficult climbing the hill, because of the moon's low gravity."

"Did you see what was going on behind the hill?" asked Mrs. Anderson.

"Yes," answered Mr. Janus. "When we got to the top of the hill, I could see that the saucer people were knocking down part of their base. They asked me to tell the people of the world their reasons for leaving. They had decided that the people on earth were not advanced enough to be welcomed into the Galaxy Federation of Intelligent Beings."

"That's too bad," Einstein said. But I can see why they felt that way, he thought. "Mom, would it be O.K. if I went outside to play now?"

"Would you excuse me for a second, Mr. Janus?" asked Mrs. Anderson. "I'll be back in a minute."

Einstein and Mrs. Anderson went outside the den. "Well, what do you think?" Mrs. Anderson asked. "Did Janus make any scientific errors?"

"As far as I can tell, just one," Einstein said. "But that error is enough of a whopper to make me think his whole story is fiction."

Can you solve the puzzle: What was the scientific error in the story of the saucer people?

"Was the error in his story that the temperature on the moon was hot enough to boil water?" Mrs. Anderson asked. "That seems wrong to me. I always thought the moon's surface was very cold."

"The moon's surface is either cold or hot," Einstein said. "Because the moon has no atmosphere, the surface temperatures are very extreme. In the shade, the temperature is lower than the coldest spot on earth. In the sun, the temperature is higher than the hottest spot here."

"Then what was the error, Adam?"

"The mistake that Janus made had to do with the lack of atmosphere on the moon," explained Einstein. "Mr. Janus said that he heard a hammering going on behind a hill. But sound must travel through air to be heard. How could Janus have heard the sound of hammering in a place that has no air?"

"Thanks, Adam. I knew I could count on you."

"Well, you can certainly count on what I expect to be in two years."

"What?" Mrs. Anderson asked.

"Fourteen," Einstein said.

"Don't press your luck," Mrs. Anderson said.

8
The Angry Bull

Every so often, Dr. Anderson would take one of his sons with him when he made calls on sick animals. Today it was Einstein's turn to accompany his father.

Einstein enjoyed seeing his dad at work. Dr. Anderson seemed to know just what to do to calm down an animal during an examination. His hands were gentle, and he worked quickly to find out what was wrong. Dr. Anderson had the reputation of being the best veterinarian in the county.

This day Dr. Anderson was visiting the Jones farm to check on some sick cows. He examined the animals and gave them some medicine. Dr. Anderson and Einstein were just about to leave when Mr. Jones stopped them.

"Doc, I wonder if you can solve a problem that Ajax, my prize bull, seems to be having," Mr. Jones said.

"What seems to be wrong with Ajax? He looked fine when I saw him a few minutes ago."

"That's just it," Mr. Jones replied. "He seems to be O.K. But whenever he's left alone, something strange happens. I come back and Ajax is all sweaty and irritable. If he keeps behaving this way, I won't be able to enter him in the county fair. Then Apollo, the bull Burns owns, will probably win the award for best bull. And there's no way that Burns's bull Apollo is better than Ajax."

"Let me take a look," said Dr. Anderson.

They went back to the yard where Ajax was penned. The bull seemed angry and nervous. But Dr. Anderson kept talking in a soothing way until he was able to examine the animal. At the end of the examination Dr. Anderson seemed puzzled.

"Ajax is in fine shape," Dr. Anderson told Mr. Jones. "But there are scratches on Ajax's back that puzzle me. I wonder if you would mind letting Adam stay with the bull this morning to observe what happens. You just go on about your chores the way you always do."

"That'd be fine," said Mr. Jones. "But will Adam know what to look for?"

"Don't worry, I'll give Adam instructions," answered Dr. Anderson.

Dr. Anderson took his son aside. "Adam, I want you to go into the barn and watch the bull pen from a window. Try not to let anyone see you. I'll be back before lunchtime to pick you up, and you can tell me if anything happens."

Einstein thought the instructions were a little odd, but he said he would do as his father asked.

Mr. Jones went to work in the fields and Mrs. Jones left for town to do some shopping. Einstein watched the bull, but Ajax didn't seem to be doing very much except brush off flies with his tail.

After an hour or so in the hot barn, Einstein got very drowsy. He decided to go up to the hayloft, stretch out on the hay, and watch Ajax from the window upstairs. The hay was very comfortable. In a few minutes Einstein was fast asleep.

Einstein hadn't been asleep very long when he was awakened by the sound of Ajax snorting and crashing into the fence. Einstein rushed downstairs and out of the barn.

Ajax was standing in the middle of the pen, pawing the ground with his foot and about to charge. Just outside the fence was Pat Burns, the oldest son of Farmer Burns. Pat the Brat.

"Pat, what are you doing to that bull?" Einstein called out.

Pat seemed surprised to see Einstein. "Where did you come from?" he said.

He quickly put some pebbles he was holding in his hand back into his pocket. "I'm not doing anything to that old bull," he said. "Ajax isn't as good as Apollo any day of the week. Apollo will win best-bull award hands down."

Einstein looked at Ajax. The bull was sweating badly and breathing hard. Then Einstein looked back at Pat. He said, "You've been throwing stones at him—that's why Ajax is so hot and angry. You're trying to make Mr. Jones think his bull is sick so he won't enter him in the county fair."

"That's not so," Pat said angrily. "I just walked past the bull and he got angry. And anybody can see why. It's because of the red shirt I'm wearing. When Ajax saw the red shirt, he just charged at me. It's not my fault that I'm wearing red."

"It certainly is your fault that Ajax is angry," said Einstein.

Can you solve the puzzle: How did Einstein know that Pat had done more to anger Ajax than just walk past in a red shirt?

"How can you prove that?" Pat asked. "Did you see me throw rocks at Ajax?"

"No," Einstein said, "I didn't actually see you throw rocks at Ajax. But I know there has to be another explanation."

"How do you know that?" Pat demanded.

"Because bulls are color blind," Einstein said. "All the stories you hear about bulls getting angry when they see red are just not true. Ajax didn't get angry at your red shirt. He got angry because you threw rocks at him."

Later, when Einstein rode home with his father, Dr. Anderson thanked him for being so observant.

"Oh, I knew that explanation about red shirts was just a lot of bull," Einstein answered.

Dr. Anderson groaned.

9
The Disappearing Cookies

It was only one week before school would start again. One week left to get in more swimming, ball playing, and summer fun. One week to sleep late in the morning. One week left with no homework, no studying, no tests, no report cards.

To celebrate the last week of freedom, Einstein's friends decided to have a picnic. The picnic was to be held in Big Lake State Park. The lake in the park was several miles long and almost a mile wide. Each person was assigned to bring some food, which everybody was going to share. Einstein and Margaret volunteered to bake cookies.

Einstein went over to Margaret's house the night before the picnic. Margaret answered the door and led Einstein into the kitchen. The kitchen table was loaded with flour, sugar, milk, chocolate chips —all the ingredients for the cookies they were going to bake.

"Are you going to make the table disappear like you did at Aunt Bess's house?" Einstein asked innocently.

Margaret laughed. "I'm not going to make the table disappear," she said, "but unless you start helping me I'm going to make you disappear."

"Sure, let's begin," Einstein said. "It's a good idea to light the oven now before we begin to mix the batter. The oven will take a while to heat up."

Einstein and Margaret baked one batch of chocolate chip cookies, then another batch, then another. By the time they got through baking, they had 257 cookies—enough for every eager eater in the class.

The day dawned cloudy, and it looked like rain. But they all decided to go ahead with the picnic anyway. Almost everybody in the class came, even Pat the Brat and his sidekick Herman.

Before eating, most of the kids went swimming in the lake. Einstein, Margaret, and their friends were splashing, throwing Frisbees around, and having a lot of fun.

Pat and Herman were not too happy. They had tried to duck Einstein but had not been very successful. He was a much better swimmer than either of them and easily outdistanced them when they got too close.

After swimming, Einstein and Margaret sat down to eat. A grand feast was spread out on the big picnic table: fried chicken, cold cuts, salads, watermelon, and delicious bread. There were even peanut butter and jelly sandwiches for those who ate nothing else.

They were about to start on the cookies for dessert when the rain began. The kids scurried around, looking for shelter in one place or another.

Einstein and Margaret threw a plastic sheet over the cookies to keep them from getting wet. Then they ran into the building that was used for dressing rooms.

Most of the class was in the building. The boys and girls were talking and laughing. Soon they started a game of charades.

Margaret had to act out the movie title, *Alien*. She tried to act like a monster, but nobody guessed what she was doing. Einstein thought she was the monster of Frankenstein. Someone else said she looked more like Pat going after Einstein in the water.

It got darker and darker. It was difficult to see outside in the rain. Just as it looked as if the rain were going to continue the rest of the day, the clouds began to break up and the rain stopped.

The sun broke through and the charade players went outside. The ground was soaked, and the ball field looked muddy.

"Don't leave until you eat our cookies," Margaret said. "They're delicious."

"That's right," Einstein added. "Those cookies are the best I ever baked."

"*Who* ever baked?" asked Margaret with that look in her eyes.

"*We* ever baked," Einstein said with a laugh.

They went over to the table, but the cookies were gone. Nothing lay beneath the plastic sheet except a few crumbs.

"Who took the cookies?" said Einstein. He looked over at Pat and Herman, who were standing near the table and trying to keep from laughing. "Did you take them, Pat?" Einstein asked.

"Who—me?" Pat said with his best innocent face. "Not a chance. Do you know who took them, Herman?"

"Sure," Herman answered. "I saw who took them. It was a bear that came out of the woods. Pat and I were staying under the trees during the rain. You couldn't see a thing, it was so dark and rainy. I heard this loud crash of thunder and turned in time to see a bolt of lightning hit a tree across the lake. I saw the bear taking the cookies during the lightning flash. Then it got dark again and I didn't see where it went."

"I don't believe you," Margaret said. "You took these cookies and hid them someplace."

"I don't care what you believe," Pat said. "I saw the same thing that Herman saw. And you or Einstein can't prove I didn't."

"Oh, yes, I can," Einstein said. "You and Herman are lying."

Can you solve the puzzle: How can Einstein prove that Herman and Pat were lying?

"Don't tell me you saw us take the cookies," Pat said.

"I didn't see you take the cookies," Einstein said, "but I know you are not telling the truth about seeing the bear take them."

"How do you know that?" Pat demanded.

"I have to explain a little science for you to understand," Einstein said. "You see, a flash from a bolt of lightning travels at the speed of light, 186,000 miles per second. It would travel the mile distance across the lake in just a tiny fraction of a second."

"So what?" said Herman.

"Just pay attention and you'll see," answered Einstein. "Light travels fast, but sound travels much slower, only about 1100 feet a second. That means that the sound of thunder would take about five seconds to travel across the lake."

Margaret nodded. "You're right, Einstein. Now I see it," she said.

Pat shook his head. "I don't see what lightning and thunder have to do with cookies," he complained.

"Just this," Einstein said. "Herman said that he heard a crash of thunder and turned just in time to see a lightning bolt strike a tree across a mile-wide lake. But that's impossible. Herman wouldn't have heard the thunder till five seconds *after* he saw the lightning. He must have been lying about seeing the bear take the cookies in the flash of lightning. Maybe these bare facts will enlighten him."

10
The Science of
Baseball Throwing

After Pat brought back the cookies that he had hidden (see The Disappearing Cookies), he said that he had been only kidding. He really had been going to bring back the cookies all along.

"I just wanted to see if Einstein could solve the puzzle," Pat said. But you could tell by the look on Pat's face as he spoke that Einstein was not exactly his favorite person.

"Right, Pat, let's forget about the cookies," Einstein said good-naturedly. "Why don't we just get on with the picnic? Maybe we can play ball."

"The ball field is too muddy for our softball

game," said Margaret. "But we can have a catch or play running bases."

"Sure, why don't we have a catch?" Pat said. "Come on, Einstein, just to show you there's no hard feelings, I'll have a catch with you."

Pat and Einstein got their gloves and walked over to a place on the field that was a little drier than the rest. Margaret and some of the others followed.

"I'll pitch and you catch," Pat said. "This'll be home plate." He pointed to a patch of grass. "You stay there and I'll loosen up the old arm and burn a few in."

Einstein agreed, but he had a sinking feeling about what was to come. Sure enough, Pat began to burn in his fast ball. He pitched harder and harder.

Einstein caught most of them, but his hand began to sting with the speed of the ball.

Finally Einstein spoke up. "Pat," he said, "I think it's my turn to burn in a few. You catch and I'll pitch."

"Einstein," Pat said with a sneer, "you don't have a fast ball. Your best pitch can hardly knock over a blade of grass."

Pat and Einstein changed positions on the field. Einstein started to pitch to Pat. But try as hard as he could, Einstein's arm was just not as strong as Pat's. His fast ball just did not have the same zip. After a while Einstein stopped throwing and walked back to Pat.

"Well, I'm glad we had this throw together," said Einstein. "After all, school starts next week and it's back to the books," he added.

"Oh, sure," Pat said with a laugh. "You can beat me when it comes to science or books, but that's just school work. I'd like to see you beat me when it comes to throwing or something like that. What good is science then?"

"You can use science anyplace," answered Einstein, "even in sports. Let me think."

Einstein pushed his glasses back on his nose. After a minute he said, "I've got it."

"What have you got, Einstein," Pat asked, "besides a weak arm?"

"We'll see about that, Pat," Einstein replied. "How about a contest? A throwing contest?"

"Are you kidding?" Pat's mouth dropped open in surprise. "You want to have a throwing contest? Me and you? What do I have to do, throw the ball with my left hand?"

"No, you can throw the ball with your right hand. But there is one condition," Einstein said.

"What's that?" Pat asked.

"The contest will be to see who can throw the ball farther. To make it fair, *you* have to throw the ball straight ahead on a line, not up into the air."

"And how are you going to throw it, Einstein? With a cannon?"

"Oh, no," Einstein said. "I'm just going to use my arm and nothing else. I'll throw the ball from the same spot you do. We'll each get one chance, and I'll bet my throw goes farther."

Can you solve the puzzle: What does Einstein know about throwing a ball that will help him beat Pat?

The baseball throwing contest proved to be no contest. No matter how hard Pat threw the ball on a straight line, Einstein was able to throw the ball farther.

Finally Pat turned to Einstein and said, "I don't understand why the way you throw the ball has anything to do with how far it goes."

"It's all a matter of gravity," Einstein said.

"You mean what goes up must come down?" Pat asked.

"Yes," Einstein said, "about the only thing that goes up and doesn't come down is your age." He laughed at his joke.

Margaret didn't laugh. "Space rockets sometimes don't come down," she said.

"But baseballs do," Einstein said. "Gravity will pull down any ball you throw or hit. If you throw the ball straight out in a flat line the way Pat did, gravity will pull it down to the ground before it goes very far."

"But if you throw the ball straight up," Margaret said, "it will come down close to you."

"That's right," Einstein said. "So the answer is to throw the ball exactly midway between straight out and straight up. You have to throw the ball at a forty-five-degree angle."

"What's that?" asked Pat.

"The corner of a book is a ninety-degree angle,"

answered Einstein. "A line going right through the middle of the corner makes a forty-five-degree angle with either edge of the book."

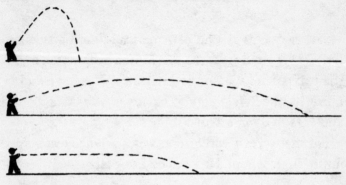

"So what?" said Pat.

"That's the angle a person usually throws a ball at when he wants it to go far," said Einstein.

"You mean like from the outfield to home plate?" Margaret asked.

Einstein nodded.

"Well, I usually play first base," muttered Pat as he walked away.

"That's funny," said Einstein to Margaret. "He always *seems* to be out in left field."

SEYMOUR SIMON is one of America's leading science writers for young readers. Mr. Simon has written more than sixty books, among which are *The Secret Clocks*, *Look to the Night Sky*, *The Paper Airplane Book*, and *Pets in a Jar*, all for Viking.

For many years Mr. Simon was a science teacher in junior high school. He lives on Long Island.